THIS BOOK BELONGS TO:

WHAT MAKES YOU HAPPY? DRAW IT!

SAMMIE
THE SUPPORT SHEPHERD

WRITTEN BY: D.R. GALLARDO

ILLUSTRATED BY: SARAH BUSBEE

A HEALTHY STRONG AND SMART BOOK

P.O. BOX 1578
SPRING VALLEY, CA 91979

SAMMIE THE SUPPORT SHEPHERD

BOOKS MADE IN THE USA.
Our books are available to order in bulk for promotional, educational or business use.
Contact support@healthystrongandsmart.com for inquiries.

Library of Congress Control Number: 2021913862
FIRST EDITION

ISBN 978-1-7344002-3-6
ISBN 978-1-7344002-4-3 (Spanish Translation)

Illustrated by Sarah Busbee
Design by Briana Gallardo
Edited by Christopher Lee

WITH LOVE.

FOR SANDY, RYAN & BRITTANY.

Swimming tones up your MUSCLES and increases strength.

Your Body extended at its full length.

Improves CIRCULATION!
Escalates CONCENTRATION!

SAMMIE SAYS, "SWIMMING IS BEST WHEN SWIMMING WITH MATES."

CHILDREN LAUGHING! KIDS AT PLAY.
DEEP BREATHING! DEEP BREATHING!
A MINDFUL WAY.

INSIDE YOUR BODY AND INSIDE YOUR BRAIN,
OXYGEN TRAVELS THROUGHOUT YOUR VEINS.

SAMMIE SAYS, "YOUR HEART AND LUNGS NEED OXYGEN, TOO!" BEING ACTIVE IS IMPORTANT FOR YOU!

Sammie says, "Don't be afraid of the monkey bar rungs. It's good for your muscles and great for your LUNGS!"

Ropes and rock climbing! Hours of fun.
Enjoyable PLAYTIME. A day in the sun!

From joyful laughter, all muscles **RELAX**.

Sammie says, "Be sure to drink water and eat HEALTHY snacks."

A GIGGLE WILL BOOST AND STRENGTHEN YOUR HEART.
A CARDIO WORKOUT, A MID-DAY RESTART.
FROM LAUGHTER, CLEAR CHOICES, A MORE CLEVER MIND.
SAMMIE SAYS, "LAUGHTER IS KEY FOR ALL OF MANKIND!"

Sammie says, "Gaze towards the sky for a time well spent."

It keeps a **MIND** happy, amused, and content.

TREASURE OUR MOON, THE STARS, ALL PLANETS ABOVE.

LEAVE A POSITIVE IMPRESSION.
YOUR SIGNATURE OF LOVE.

Your eyes and hands through the POWER of play are developing skills.

PRACTICE each day!

THROWING AND CATCHING KEEPS A **BRAIN** FIT.

Footballs and Frisbees! EXCITING and fun!

All playing TOGETHER under the sun.

SAMMIE SAYS, "FUN IN THE PARK OR ON A BEACH, CREATES **CHEERFUL** MEMORIES THE MIND WILL KEEP."

A WALK THROUGH THE PARK OR WHEREVER YOU START,
WILL IMPROVE YOUR BRAIN AND ALSO YOUR HEART.

SAMMIE SAYS, "YOUR THYROID AND MUSCLES WILL BENEFIT, TOO!"

A FRESH SEA BREEZE HAS POSITIVE VALUE.

Pet Shop

BREAK TIME!!

WHERE IS YOUR FAVORITE PLACE TO WALK?
A BEACH? A PARK? WHERE WILL YOU START?

Walking and talking at a fast pace
often turns into—a **RACE!"**

Sammie says, "Happiness from a lively walk,
is sharing FRIENDSHIP, LAUGHTER, and TALK."

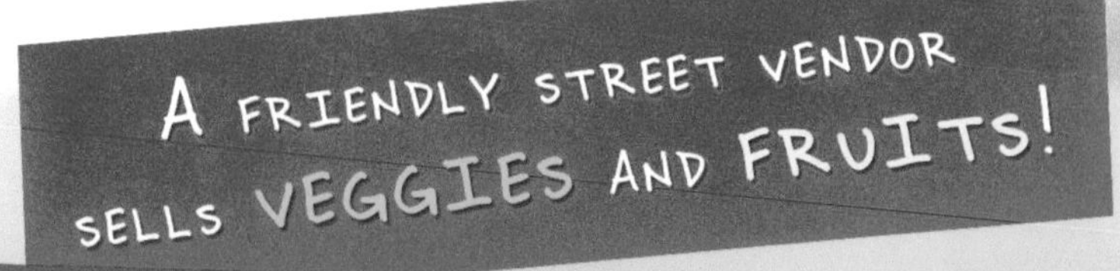

SAMMIE SAYS, "HEALTHY SNACK TIME HAS NO SUBSTITUTE!"

Apples! Carrots! Pack ENERGY inside.
Each a treat before a bicycle ride.
FRUITS & VEGGIES

Bicycle RIDING is fun and exciting!

It's also a FOCUSING tool.

SAMMIE SAYS, "RIDING YOUR BIKE **BENEFITS** YOUR BRAIN!"

IT WILL HELP YOU DO BETTER IN SCHOOL.

SANDCASTLES! BEACH ART!
A TON OF FUN!!

ENJOY WITH FRIENDS AND ALL YOUR LOVED ONES.

PIVOTING TO THE LEFT, AND THEN TO THE RIGHT!

SAMMIE SAYS, "MY WAVERING STEPS CREATE ENDLESS DELIGHT!"

WHETHER SPRINTING OR RUNNING,
YOU USE THE SAME MUSCLES.

INSIDE YOUR BODY, THERE IS NEVER A TUSSLE.

When jogging TOGETHER, you use the same motions.

Sammie says, "When we run side by side, along the blue OCEAN!"

Playtime and laughter under the sun.

Surfing and KAYAKs
are oodles of fun.

Sammie says, "I love the water, paddle boarding is cool."

Fun at the beach! Watersports rule.

FROM THE DECK OF A SAILBOAT, ONE MAY NOTE,
KIDS ONBOARD WILL LEARN AS THEY FLOAT!

SAMMIE SAYS, "SAILING THE SEA
PROMOTES A PRESENCE OF MIND."
A MARITIME ADVENTURE.
WHO KNOWS WHAT YOU'LL FIND?"

After hours upon hours blanketed by sun,
laughter and talk, ends the day's fun.

Twilight waves. The sounds of the sea.
Seagulls soar softly upon a tranquil sea breeze.

BE CONFIDENT AND BRAVE IN ALL THAT YOU DO.

SAMMIE SAYS, "MY TRUSTED SUPPORT IS ALWAYS WITH YOU."

CPSIA information can be obtained
at www.ICGtesting.com
Printed in the USA
LVHW070814161121
703360LV00005B/21

* 9 7 8 1 7 3 4 4 0 0 2 3 6 *